The Flyaway Kite

BY STEVE BJÖRKMAN

WaterBrook
PRESS

THE FLYAWAY KITE
Published by WaterBrook Press
5446 North Academy Boulevard, Suite 200
Colorado Springs, Colorado 80918
A division of Random House, Inc.

Scripture taken from the *Holy Bible, New International Version*®.
NIV®. Copyright © 1973, 1978, 1984 by International Bible Society.
Used by permission of Zondervan Publishing House. All rights reserved.

ISBN 1-57856-264-3

Printed in the United States of America
2000—First Edition

10 9 8 7 6 5 4 3 2 1

For Noel Stookey—

The Light you reflect

has influenced me greatly.

Thank you.

—S.B.

The little red kite felt handsome!
It was so proud of its shiny fresh
paint. A gentle tug from the boy
who had made the kite reminded it
of the string that connected them.

From the very beginning it flew
higher and better than any kite
ever. Looping, zooming, climbing,
or diving, the kite loved to fly
anywhere the boy directed.

The kite knew the boy loved it, too. Every day they would have a new adventure. Sometimes the kite flew so high it nearly disappeared into the sky. Other times it flew so fast it would chase the birds right through the clouds.

After a while though, the little kite began to tire of these tricks. "I don't like this string," it said to itself. "I don't want to be controlled by the boy. I want to be free."

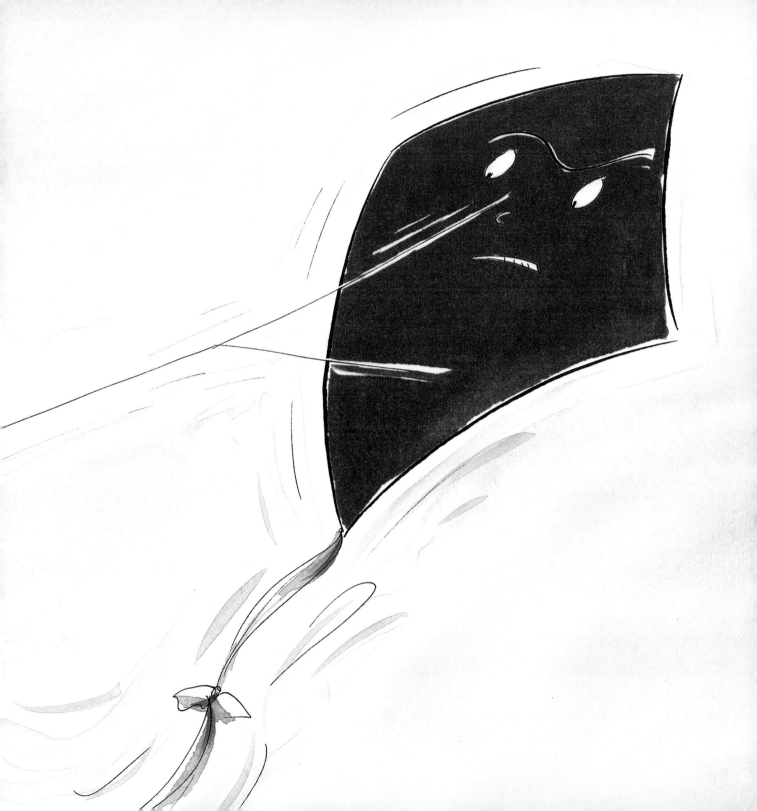

The kite began to pull and tug at the
string that connected it to the boy.
Finally the string broke, and the kite
was carried away with the wind.

"I'm free! I'm free!" it shouted.

But the little kite didn't fly or loop or zoom like it had expected. To its great surprise, the kite discovered it wasn't really free after all. You see, kites can't fly unless they're connected to their owners by a string. It just fell from the sky, blowing wherever the wind took it.

But the boy followed.

"Oh no!" the kite said as it crashed into the top of a jagged stone mountain.

The boy climbed the mountain, but the wind blew the kite away.

"Help!" it cried as it tumbled down through the snow and rocks and was caught high in a scraggly tree.

The boy climbed the tree, but the wind tore the kite from the branches.

"Ouch!" the kite shrieked as an eagle snatched it up and began to rip off pieces to use for its nest.

The boy came upon the eagle just as the wind took what was left of the kite and tossed it over a cliff.

"Save me!" the kite gurgled as it was thrown headfirst into a rushing river. It rolled over and over and smashed against the boulders.

The boy followed the kite, but it was washed far out to sea.

Cold and frightened, the little kite
sank deep into the ocean.

The boy dived down to get the kite,
but a shark carried it away.

A fisherman caught the shark and saw
the kite. He just laughed at the sight and
threw the ragged thing away.

The battered kite sighed with relief
when the boy found it in a Dumpster.
He carried it home. "You are safe again,
little kite," he said. "I have you now."

The weak and tired kite lay quietly on the workbench as the boy carefully cleaned off the seaweed and slime. It was comforted by the boy's loving hands as he patched and repaired it.

Step by step, the little kite began to feel beautiful once again.

When the work was done, the boy carried the little red kite up to their favorite hill and said to it, "I made you to fly high and free, my little kite, and as long as you stay connected to me, you always will."

With a gentle tug on the string, the kite floated up into the breezy sky.

If you had been a bird flying by
and had listened very carefully,
you would have heard the little
kite answer the boy and say,
"Yes! This is just where I belong."

Where can I go from your Spirit?

Where can I flee from your presence?

If I go up to the heavens,

you are there;

if I make my bed in the depths, you are there.

If I rise on the wings of the dawn,

if I settle on the far side of the sea,

even there your hand

will guide me,

your right hand will hold me fast.

PSALM 139:7-10